ADDY'S
SUMMER PLACE

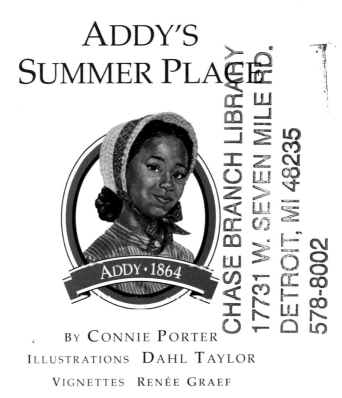

ADDY · 1864

BY CONNIE PORTER
ILLUSTRATIONS DAHL TAYLOR
VIGNETTES RENÉE GRAEF

THE AMERICAN GIRLS COLLECTION®

Published by Pleasant Company Publications
Copyright © 2003 by Pleasant Company
For information, address: Book Editor, Pleasant Company Publications,
8400 Fairway Place, P.O. Box 620998, Middleton, WI 53562.

Visit our Web site at **americangirl.com**

Printed in Singapore.
03 04 05 06 07 08 09 10 TWP 10 9 8 7 6 5 4 3 2 1

Library of Congress Cataloging-in-Publication Data

Porter, Connie Rose, 1959–
Addy's summer place / by Connie Porter ;
illustrations, Dahl Taylor ; vignettes, Renée Graef.
p. cm. — (The American girls collection)
Summary: In 1866, eleven-year-old Addy and her family gather
in Cape Island, later known as Cape May, New Jersey, where she
encounters an impoverished white girl who treats her badly.
ISBN 1-58485-697-1 (HC)
1. African Americans—Juvenile fiction. [1. African Americans—Fiction.
2. Race relations—Fiction. 3. Cape May (N.J.)—History—19th century—Fiction.]
I. Taylor, Dahl, ill. II. Graef, Renée, ill. III. Title. IV. Series.
PZ7.P825 Adi 2003
[Fic]—dc21 2002029669

The AMERICAN GIRLS COLLECTION®

PICTURE CREDITS

The following individuals and organizations have generously given permission to reprint illustrations contained in "Looking Back": p. 34—John Crino Collection/Archive Photos; p. 35—Jane Dixon collection; p. 36—Haynes Foundation Collection, Montana Historical Society; p. 37—From the collections of Henry Ford Museum & Greenfield Village (43-A-80 *(Detail)*); p. 38—American (New Castle, DE) bathing suit c. 1855, Philadelphia Museum of Art (53-57-6a, b); p. 39—© Dave G. Houser/CORBIS; p. 40—photo by George E. Thomas; p. 41—John Thomas Nash and Janet Davidson Nash African-American History Archives of the Center for Community Arts, Cape May, N.J.

TABLE OF CONTENTS

POPPA
*Addy's father, whose
dream gives the family
strength.*

MOMMA
*Addy's mother, whose
love helps the family
survive.*

ADDY
*A courageous girl,
smart and strong,
growing up during
the Civil War.*

SAM
Addy's seventeen-year-old brother, determined to be free.

ESTHER
Addy's three-year-old sister.

SARAH MOORE
Addy's good friend.

ADDY'S SUMMER PLACE

A ddy, Addy, Addy," Addy's little sister, Esther, called to her. Each time she said her name, Esther tapped Addy sharply, like a pesky woodpecker. Addy didn't feel like playing, so she ignored Esther's pecking and chattering and fixed her gaze out the window of the train. She, Momma, and Esther were heading to Cape Island, New Jersey, for the Fourth of July holiday.

Addy had always wanted to ride a train. Now here she was inside this

1

clattering, smoke-breathing machine flying faster than a bird! Bits of ash sailed in through the open windows of this car for black people. Outside, the world rushed by—woods thick with trees, farmers driving teams of mules, meadows of uncountable wildflowers, and black flocks of crows thick as storm clouds, wheeling over fields of corn.

Addy had thought she and her brother, Sam, would spend the Fourth watching fireworks at the harbor after he got home from work. But Momma had surprised Addy with the news that they were going for three days to Cape Island. Poppa had been working there all summer helping build a hotel for the railroad, and the railroad had given him passes so the rest of the family could come visit.

Momma had made Addy and Esther new dresses for the trip, and for the first time in Addy's life, Momma had curled Addy's hair on paper rollers. Addy liked the feeling of the spiral curls bouncing in the breeze. She pulled at a few curls and felt them spring back into place.

"That wind is going to whip the curls right out of your head," said Momma as she closed their window.

Addy thought that with all the curling wax and lard Momma had used to set her hair, her curls could survive a hurricane, but she didn't want to contradict Momma.

"Can't we leave it open some?" asked Addy. "If too many people close the windows, it's going to be hot as blazes in here."

Momma let Addy open the window just a crack and gave Addy and Esther their lunch—meat pies wrapped in napkins.

"I'm too excited to eat!" declared Addy.

"I'm too 'cited to eat," said Esther, who sat happily munching her pie.

Addy smiled at her sister and told Momma, "Part of me feel like I want the train to go slower so I can see everything there is to see, but part of me wish it was faster so I could get to see Poppa quicker.

Momma, you ever feel like that? Like you was going some place too fast and too slow all at the same time?"

Momma smoothed a few strands of hair that had come loose from her bun before she said, "I can't rightly say so. There's been places I wanted to rush to, and then there's been others I didn't care if I got to 'til June-vember."

Addy giggled. "*June-vember?* There ain't no such month."

Smiling, Momma said, "Sure there is, baby. You'll understand soon enough."

"Well, I hope we get to Cape Island soon," said Addy. "I know it's going to be beautiful." She closed her eyes and pictured a sky the color of robins' eggs and air so sweet, you'd think you were in heaven. She imagined herself staying in one of the grand hotels overlooking the sea. She'd float into sleep in a feather bed as soft as a cloud and awake as the morning sun kissed her cheek. Addy knew her family couldn't afford to stay in such a place. They would stay at the camp near Poppa's work site. But on such a beautiful day, it seemed right to hold on to a beautiful dream.

☀

When the train pulled into the Cape Island station, Addy was the first to spot Poppa. Dressed in his Sunday clothes, he looked handsome and strong,

*When the train pulled into the Cape Island station,
Addy was the first to spot Poppa.*

his face bright with joy. Addy dropped her bag and rushed into his arms.

"Wait a minute," Poppa said, pulling back to look at her. "I left my two little girls in Philadelphia. I see one coming up yonder, but who is this looking all growed up?"

"You know it's me, Poppa," Addy giggled.

Poppa laughed, and he and Addy walked back down the platform to Esther and Momma. Gathering their bags, they headed to a wagon Poppa had borrowed from his boss. Poppa said, "We going to make a stop before we go to the camp."

"Where we going, Poppa?" asked Esther.

"I'd like to know myself," said
Momma. "I need to get to the camp to
get supper started."

"Well," said Poppa, "I couldn't have
y'all come here looking this fine and not
give y'all a taste of the good life. We going
to the Banneker House for ice cream."

Addy jumped a foot off the ground.
"Do you really mean it, Poppa?" she
asked. Addy had heard about the elegant
guest house where wealthy black people
could spend the night or eat dinner in the
fancy dining room.

"I sure do," said Poppa. "That is,
unless y'all don't want to go."

Addy looked at Momma pleadingly.

"I guess we got time to go and set a

while," Momma said.

The Banneker House was grand. The dining room walls were covered in floral paper, and the curtains were the color of fresh butter. The tablecloths were snow white, and a vase of flowers sat on the sideboard. Master Stevens's house hadn't been this fine, and he was white *and* a slave holder. Addy savored every sweet, cold spoonful of ice cream.

When she finished, Addy told Poppa, "You know, they opened a colored ice cream parlor back home called J.J. Lyons. How about when your job over, all of us go—Sam, too?"

"Sound good to me," said Poppa. "It's about time there was one for colored

folks. We need to start building more of our own places."

Refolding her napkin neatly into thirds, Addy said thoughtfully, "Poppa, everyone talking these days about the Reconstruction, how the country being put back *together* after the war. Then why colored folks and white folks got to always

11

have a *separate* place for everything?"

"I don't know," Poppa replied.
"Maybe only God know the answer to that."

☀

From the camp, Addy could see the
huge five-story hotel that Poppa was
working on. Its wooden frame looked
like the skeleton of a gigantic beast. The
camp itself was up a slope from the ocean
on the edge of a deep woods. Poppa and
the other workers were living in lean-tos
with canvas flaps for doors. There was an
outdoor kitchen with a rough-hewn
table, a battered cookstove, and
a fire pit dug into the ground.
A privy sat at the far end of the

privy

12

clearing. Poppa had built a lean-to a small distance into the woods so that the family could have some privacy.

Addy quickly changed into her work shift so she could go with Poppa to check his rabbit traps. She hadn't been in the woods since leaving the plantation in North Carolina. As she padded down a trail of pine needles, Addy realized how much she missed the woods. There was a hushed beauty here, the soft light shining through branches, the songs of birds, the soothing smell of pine. Philadelphia, with its scorching summer heat, smoky air, and rush of people, seemed a world away.

The first trap Addy and Poppa came to had not been sprung. The next two held fat brown rabbits. Addy looked away as Poppa cut the dead rabbits loose.

She, Poppa, and Sam had rarely had time to trap and fish back in North Carolina, but when they did, Addy could never stand looking at what they caught. She felt sorry for the trapped animals, but she had eaten them, grateful for any meal that would fill her stomach for a while.

The last trap she and Poppa came to had been sprung. It held bits of fur and some blood, but no rabbit.

"I'm sure of it now," Poppa said. "Somebody been stealing from my traps."

Kneeling down next to the trap, Addy asked Poppa, "Who?"

Poppa got down on his knees and

started cleaning out the trap. "I don't know," he said. "I suspects whoever doing it is hungry."

"Whoever doing it a thief," said Addy. "If they hungry, why don't they set their own traps?"

"Might not have any," Poppa said, busily working. "Not everybody got money like them people seaside. There's people got little of nothing. Rich folks moving in left and right, building houses and hotels on the shore. Poor folks done had to get out the way."

"That don't sound fair," said Addy.

Poppa said, "No, it ain't, but the only reason I got a job here is because of all the building. There ain't jobs for everybody, though, and that leaves folks bitter. Colored workers ain't really welcome here. White folks think we taking their jobs."

Addy thought about Poppa's words as they started back into the woods. She wondered how anyone could hold on to bitterness in such a peaceful place.

Back at the camp, Momma asked Addy and Esther to fetch water from the nearby stream. Esther held Addy's hand for a short while, but then she pulled away. Bounding ahead, Esther began pinching off the yellow heads of dandelions, blowing  the seeds off the white seed balls, and chasing after a butterfly she had no hope of catching.

When they reached the stream, Esther busily picked purple phlox while Addy got the water. Addy glanced upstream and noticed a thin white girl about her age along with a little boy about Esther's age. They both had bright red curly hair and dirt-streaked faces. The girl was fishing, so Addy dipped her bucket into the water quietly. When the bucket was full, Addy looked up to see that the boy had wandered over. He asked Esther her name.

"Her name Esther," said Addy as Esther smiled shyly at the boy. Esther offered the boy one of her flowers, and as he reached for it, Addy saw the girl storming toward them.

"You better stop talking to colored people before you get me in trouble!" the girl screamed, snatching the boy's arm and swatting him hard on the behind.

"Hey, you ain't got to hit him like that," Addy said.

Dragging her screaming brother behind her, the girl turned and gave Addy a burning, hateful glare. "Don't you step out of your place with me, colored girl!" the girl spat. "You better go back to where you belong." Then she turned to her brother. "Stop acting like a baby. If Ma was here and seen you, she'd give you worse than I give you," the girl said.

Addy grabbed Esther's hand protectively and led her back to the trail. She could hear

"Don't you step out of your place with me, colored girl!"
the girl spat.

19

the boy's crying, muffled by the trees, and she felt sorry for him.

"That girl was bad," Esther said.

"She was downright mean," said Addy, testily, "and I hope she ain't catchin' any fish and don't have nothing for supper! That would serve her right."

☀

After a supper of fried rabbit and hoe cakes swimming in gooey, dark cane syrup, Poppa went to set his traps while Addy helped Momma clean up. Then Momma carried a sleeping Esther to the lean-to. As Addy dressed for bed, she told Momma about the redheaded girl.

"Why she have to say something like

that to me, Momma? Remind me that I'm colored and she white, like I don't know that," said Addy.

Momma sat down with Addy on a pallet she had unrolled. "Addy, I ain't going to say that girl was right. But now that you growing up, you is going to have to remember to stay in your place."

"Why colored people got a place we got to stay in?" asked Addy, angrily.

Momma looked into the darkness for a long time before she began speaking softly. "When I was coming up, I played with white children on the plantation. We was friends, making mud pies and nursing rag babies. But things was different when we started growing up. Then they was white and free, and I was colored and a slave."

"Slavery over, Momma. Things supposed to be changed," said Addy.

"They ain't changed that much," said Momma. "Whites and coloreds still keep to they own when they get a certain age, and you at that age. So if you see that white girl tomorrow, steer clear of her."

As Momma tied a sleep scarf on Addy's head, Addy could see tears glistening in Momma's eyes. "I wish things could be different for you," Momma sighed. "But this ain't my world to change." She tucked a strand of hair under Addy's scarf. "Now, would you look at these curls, already drooping in the muggy air."

"I'm sick of fussing about my hair,"

said Addy. "It's too much hard work trying to be a young lady."

"What you want to be, a baby?" asked Momma.

Addy looked at Esther, sleeping peacefully on the pallet, as if she didn't have a care in the world. "Maybe I do," said Addy softly.

After Momma left the lean-to, Addy stared into the darkness, listening to the distant sound of fireworks. *It's the Fourth of July*, Addy remembered. *But it feel more like June-vember.* She shivered and snuggled in closer beside her little sister.

☀

The next morning, Addy and Esther helped Momma pick blueberries to make a pie. It took them all morning, and Esther ate more than she picked.

Later in the day, while the pie was cooling and Esther and Momma were napping in the lean-to, Addy decided to go check Poppa's traps. As she slipped into the woods, Addy told herself firmly, *I'll be brave and look at them rabbits when I take them from the traps.*

The first snare Addy came to was empty, and she was partly relieved. Just before she reached the next trap, Addy heard a twig snap. Peering through the branches of a small pine tree, Addy saw the redheaded girl kneeling over the trap and removing the rabbit.

"Hey, that's our rabbit!" yelled Addy.

Startled, the girl dropped the rabbit and ran. Addy picked it up and took off after the girl, jumping over fallen trees, dodging tree branches, and skidding on leaves wet with dew. Addy ran fast, but this girl ran faster, as if she knew her way. Just when Addy was within arm's length of the girl, Addy tripped over a clump of roots. She took a hard fall and dropped the rabbit. Addy got up and kept running, but she could no longer see or hear the girl.

Addy's heart raced—she didn't know

where she was. *I should've listened to Momma*, she thought. *I'm lost. I just know it.* Then she heard voices. She followed them down a narrow path that ended in a clearing. Addy saw the little redheaded boy playing in front of a small cabin. The windowless cabin looked like Addy's family's cabin on the plantation.

Addy spotted the redheaded girl coming out of the woods on the other side of the cabin. She looked sweaty and tired, but she was carrying a big log. She put it on a stump and started splitting it.

The first blow just sent the log rolling to the ground. The girl stood the log back up and swung the axe again, but had no better luck. Just then, Addy saw a woman appear at the door of the cabin.

"You can't ever do a thing right!" said the woman as she bolted out of the cabin and pushed the girl aside. "What'd you catch for supper?"

"No-nothing," the girl stammered.

"Then that'll be what we all eat tonight. Nothing!" hollered the woman. "Go get the baby!"

The girl stepped away as her mother split the log with the first blow. Addy thought the girl was going to pick up her brother, but she went inside the cabin and came out with a baby who was crying and dressed in a dirty shift.

Moving away silently, Addy followed the narrow path back toward Poppa's traps. She prayed, *God, I'm sorry for hoping that girl was hungry. Please let me find that rabbit.* She searched through beds of pine needles and drifts of dried leaves until she found the rabbit she'd dropped. Addy went back to the clearing and, seeing no one outside the cabin, snuck to the tree stump and left the rabbit. As she ran back to the camp, she thought, *Maybe that girl would've never been my friend, but when she see that rabbit, she'll know I ain't her enemy.*

✷

After supper, Poppa went back to work, and Addy, Momma, and Esther

walked to the sea to bathe. Addy liked
the feel of the sand, sometimes
warm, sometimes cool, under
her bare feet. She'd gone bare-
foot on the plantation, but she couldn't
walk in Philadelphia without shoes.

Addy waded into the cooling waves,
enjoying the sound and power of them as
they rushed toward the shore. In up to her
waist, she turned and saw that Momma
had wet her feet in the water. She was
holding Esther.

Addy reached out for Esther, but she
clung tight to Momma.

"She scared," Momma said.

"Ain't nothing to be scared of," said
Addy as she walked in deeper.

"That's far enough," Momma called
to Addy.

"I'm all right," Addy said. "Don't
worry about me."

Then she turned her back to the
shore, slipped into the water, and glided,
her arms outstretched. For a few
moments, she was free under the water.

Like a bird, she felt as if she were flying.

When Addy came up for air, Momma was shaking her head. "Child, your hair's a mess!" she said. "I guess you ain't ready to be a young lady yet."

Addy turned to gaze at the ocean, sweeping out as far as she could see. "Not just yet," she said to herself. "I think I'll stay right here for a while." Then she left Momma and Esther behind and rushed back into the sea—a place deep, blue, and big enough for everyone.

CONNIE PORTER

At 9   *Now*

My mother grew up in Alabama in the 1930s, when blacks and whites went to different schools, drank from different water fountains, and sat in different places on the bus. But things slowly changed. My parents raised me and my siblings in a world that Addy's parents could only dream of—one where our "place" was of our own choosing.

Connie Porter is the author of the Addy books in The American Girls Collection.

LOOKING BACK 1864

A PEEK INTO THE PAST

CAPE ISLAND IN 1864

In the summer of 1863, railroad service
was established between Philadelphia and
Cape Island, New Jersey (later known as
Cape May). Now the ocean was just a
three-and-a-half-hour train ride from Addy's
boarding house—quite an improvement
over the 12 hours the trip took
by steamboat and stagecoach.
By 1866, as railroads and rail
services improved, it cost

about $4.80 to travel round-trip from Philadelphia to Cape Island, and some working-class families could afford to take an occasional trip.

In some ways, the railroad helped bring Americans together. Most of the people who rode trains went in similar accommodations to the same destinations. But prejudices still existed in America. While train stations provided waiting rooms for white people, blacks had to wait for the train outside on the platform.

The Cape Island train station was built by the Pennsylvania Railroad in 1863.

In the 1860s, Pullman rail cars were introduced, adding a new level of elegance to train travel—for those who could afford to pay for it. These upscale sleeping and dining cars featured walnut paneling,

velvet seats, and carpeted walkways. But Addy, Esther, and Momma rode in a separate rail car at the back of the train with other black passengers.

Pullman train cars were comfortable and fancy, almost like elegant parlors.

In Addy's time, train travel was a special event that called for proper clothes and behavior. Women and girls wore their best skirts or dresses, with matching scarves and other accessories. Railroad luggage, fashioned after stagecoach trunks, was made from

Carpetbags and domed trunks were common railroad luggage items.

wood with domed tops to protect the contents. For shorter trips passengers packed "carry-on" carpetbags or round, wallpaper-covered wooden bandboxes.

Once travelers reached Cape Island, they could enjoy a new craze called sea bathing. Sea bathers waded into the ocean up to their knees and gently splashed in the water. To maintain their modesty, nineteenth-century girls wore "bathing dresses" made from ten yards of flannel or wool. A wet bathing dress would weigh as much as ten pounds! Girls who didn't have a special bathing dress wore old clothes to take a dip in the sea.

nineteenth-century bathing dress

In 1866, Cape Island had about 600 year-round residents. During July and August, the population swelled to 50,000! To accommodate the crowds, numerous hotels, boarding houses, and cottages were built. Many of the tall, narrow cottages built for wealthier visitors featured elaborate wooden decorations inspired by gingerbread or wedding cake designs, which became characteristic of the popular Victorian-style homes.

By the summer of 1866, Cape Island had 22 hotels, but only one welcomed African-American vacationers.

The Pink House,
Cape May, New Jersey

New businesses opened to serve the visitors, including stables, souvenir shops, ice-cream parlors, and photographers. Just like at home in Philadelphia, though, these businesses were for whites only.

Although few African-American families came to Cape Island to vacation in the 1860s, hundreds of workers like Poppa found work either in construction or providing some type of service to the summer guests.

The Banneker House, which Addy and her family visited for ice cream, was one of only a few establishments where

Above—The Dale Hotel opened in 1911 to serve African-American visitors to Cape May. Right— a family reunion at the Dale Hotel in 1911.

African Americans were welcome. Banned from all-white resorts, blacks began to establish their own places of recreation and amusement, though it wasn't until the turn of the century that resort vacations became common for blacks.

Ocean breezes kept Cape Island cool in the summer—and it had the widest beach on the east coast, with the softest, whitest sand.

MAKE HOMEMADE
ICE CREAM

Try some old-fashioned vanilla ice cream—
one of Addy's favorite treats!

Although Addy and her family
couldn't afford to stay at the Banneker
House, a boarding house in Cape Island
that welcomed blacks, they surely did
enjoy the creamy vanilla ice cream that
came to their table in finer china than
they'd ever seen before. You and your
friends can make your own old-fashioned
vanilla ice cream. It's as much fun to
make as it is to eat.

You Will Need:

🖐 *An adult to help you*

Ingredients

1 pint half-and-half, chilled

1½ teaspoons vanilla

⅓ cup plus 2 tablespoons sugar

Ice cubes or crushed ice

½ cup coarse gourmet salt or rock salt

Equipment

3-pound coffee can with lid

1-pound coffee can with lid

Measuring spoons

Spoon

Towel

Mittens, gloves, or oven mitts

Rubber spatula

1. Chill the coffee cans in the freezer for about a half an hour.

2. Pour the half-and-half into the small coffee can. Add the vanilla and sugar, and mix well with the spoon.

3. Place the lid on tightly, and put the small coffee can inside the larger coffee can.

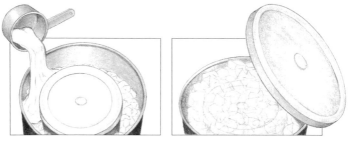

Step 4   *Step 5*

4. Starting with ice, alternate layers of ice and salt in between the 2 cans, saving some salt to cover. Be sure to shake the can a bit so the ice settles each time before adding a new layer.

5. When the layers reach the top of the small can, cover the entire lid with ice. Pour over the remaining salt. Firmly place the lid on the large can, making sure it is on tight.

6. Use the towel to wipe any excess moisture from the outside of the can. Place the can on the floor and roll or rock it gently back and forth. Put on gloves, mittens, or oven mitts if your hands get cold. It is helpful to have a friend sit on the floor so you can roll the can back and forth to each other!

7. After 10 minutes, set the large can upright, open the lid, and carefully remove the small can. Wipe the outside of the small can, making sure to

remove any salt from the outside of it,
then remove the lid.

8. Scrape the frozen ice cream from the
sides and bottom of the can with the rubber spatula or spoon, and stir the mix-
ture until it is smooth. If the ice cream
doesn't seem thick, put the top back on
and repeat step 6 for 5 more minutes. If
the ice cream still doesn't seem set, you
can put it in the freezer for 10 minutes.

Makes 2 cups.